Kids Like Me

Chloe just got home from school. As she walked into the living room, she noticed her dad hanging up the telephone. Chloe said, "Hi Daddy, who were you talking to on the phone?" Her dad replied, "It was grandma in Haiti. She would like for us to come visit her soon."

Chloe got a big smile on her face and said, "Wow, can I go too? Please! Please!" Her dad said, "You haven't been to see her since you were a little baby. Let's see what your mom says about it."

Chloe did not remember going to Haiti when she was a baby. Her mom told her that Haiti is a different country and she will need a passport to be able to go. Chloe asked, "Mom, what is a passport?" Her mom explained that a passport is a little book that shows she lives in the United States and it has a photo of Chloe with her name.

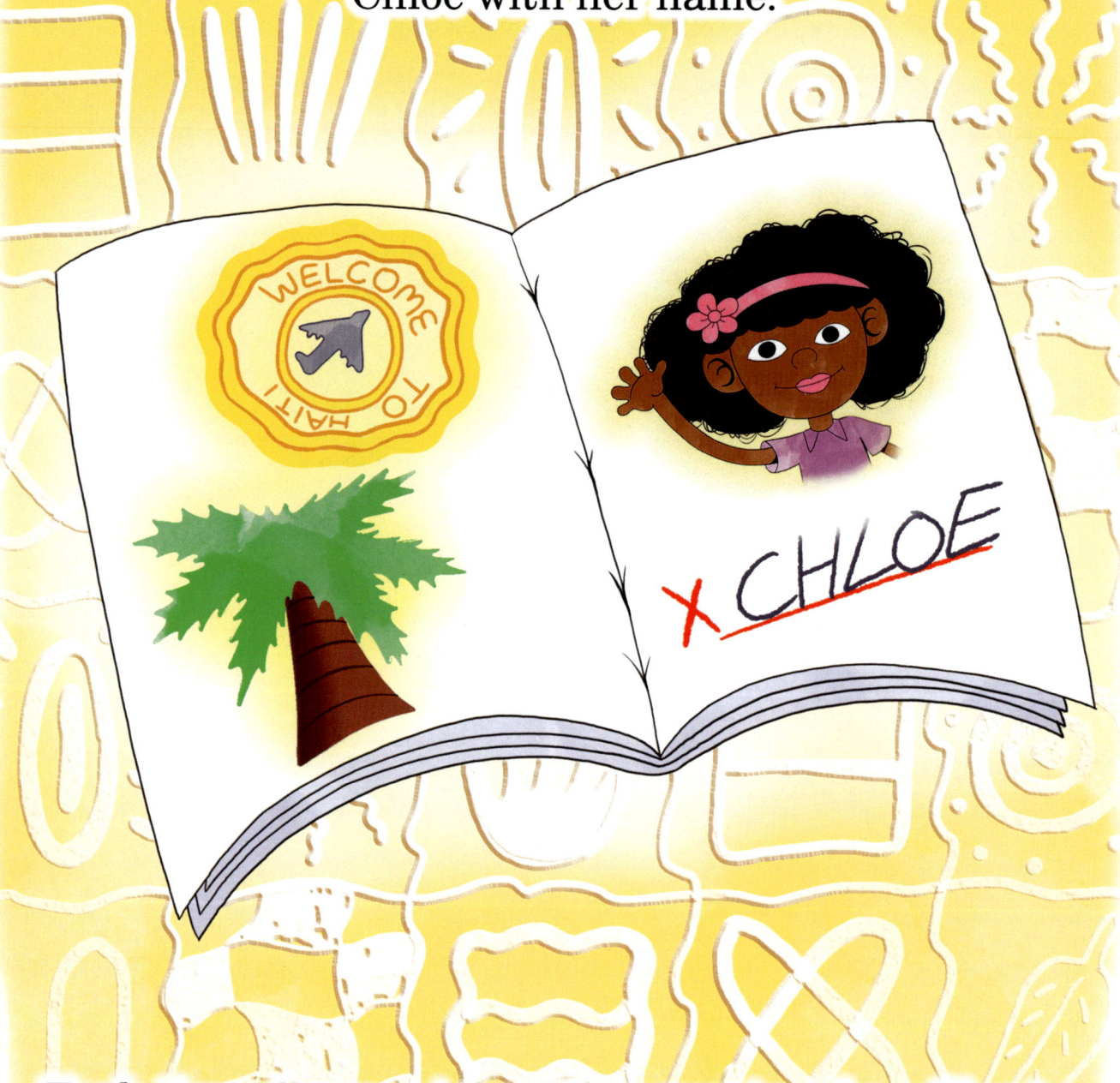

Each time she goes to another country she will get a special stamp in the book, just for that country. Some people have many different stamps in their passport books because they have traveled to many countries.

Chloe went to look for her mom and found her outside in the backyard. Chloe said, "Hi Mom, Daddy just talked with grandma and she wants us to come see her soon. Can we go? Please! Please!" Chloe's mom said, "That would be really nice. It is far away, and you will need to fly there on an airplane."

Chloe replied, "An airplane? Wow! I would love to fly on an airplane." Her mom said, "I will not be able to go this time. This will be a special trip you and Daddy take together."

The next morning as Chloe was getting ready for school, she looked at her school uniform and wondered if kids in Haiti wear uniforms to school. When Chloe got to school, she was excited to tell her friends that she would be going to visit her grandma. They asked her, "What is Haiti like?"

Chloe told them she did not remember, because she had been a little baby when she went before. She said, "My daddy says its very warm where my grandma lives, and it is near the ocean. I can't wait to see it!"

During recess, Chloe jumped rope with her friends. They loved to make up little songs to sing while jumping rope. When it was Chloe's turn to jump, she made up a song too. She sang, "One, two, three, headed to Haiti. Five, six, seven, airplane goes high as Heaven. Eight, nine, ten, going to Grandma's again."

Chloe's friends asked her if the kids in Haiti jump rope and sing songs. Chloe told them she did not know, but she would find out soon.

After school, Chloe played soccer with her friends in the neighborhood. The older kids showed her how to kick the ball into the goal. Chloe loved to play soccer after school. She told her friends that she would be going to Haiti soon to see her grandma. Her friends asked if the kids in Haiti play soccer. Chloe told them she did not know, but she would find out soon.

Later that evening, after dinner, Chloe and her mom sat at the kitchen table. Chloe had some math homework to do and her mom helped her when she had questions. Chloe liked to do math problems. She wondered if the kids in Haiti like to do math problems too, and she thought to herself, *I will find out soon.*

On Sunday morning, Chloe and her parents went to church. Chloe loved to hear the songs at church. She also loved to see her friends at church. She let them know she would be going to Haiti soon to see her grandma.

They asked if the kids in Haiti go to church. Chloe told them she did not know, but she would find out soon.

Very early the next morning, Chloe and her dad went to the airport. Chloe did not remember being on an airplane before. She was very excited. Chloe sat down in a seat by a window. Once the airplane was in the air, Chloe looked out the window and saw clouds below her.

She smiled and said, "Wow, Daddy, the clouds are below us!" Then, she looked all around and there was bright blue sky as far as she could see.

After several hours of flying, the airplane landed in Haiti.
Chloe looked out the window and it was beautiful. She said,
"Wow, Daddy, everything is so bright and sunny. Haiti is
beautiful!" Chloe could see a big mountain far away in the
background and pretty trees around the airport.

The other people on the airplane got up to leave, and
Chloe and her dad walked with them through the door and
down a little set of stairs to the ground.

As she got off the plane, Chloe noticed that things looked very different in Haiti. At first, she was a little scared and held on tight to her dad's hand. They started walking toward a little white building with a brown roof. As they got closer, there was a group of people singing songs and playing instruments. She did not understand the words they were singing.

They were singing in a different language. She asked her dad, "Why are they singing?" He replied, "They are singing to welcome us to Haiti. They are happy we are here." Chloe thought to herself, *Wow, they are so nice.*

As they walked inside the small white building, Chloe noticed her grandma was waiting across the room with a few other people. Her grandma had a big smile on her face, and she waved to Chloe. Chloe felt a little shy. She held on to her dad's hand and moved behind him. She peeked around past his leg to get a look at her grandma and gave a little smile. Everything seemed different here, and Chloe had not seen her grandma in a long time.

Before they could walk over to see her grandma, Chloe had to show her passport to a man in a uniform. The man put a stamp in Chloe's passport. Chloe looked at the stamp and it had the word: Haiti. She was excited to have a stamp for Haiti in her passport.

Chloe and her dad began walking toward Chloe's grandma. As they got closer, her grandma kneeled to the ground and stretched out her arms to give Chloe a big hug. Chloe let go of her dad's hand and hugged her grandma. Chloe smiled and no longer felt shy. She said, "I am so happy to see you Grandma."

She held her grandma's hand and they walked outside to her grandma's car.

As they were driving toward her grandma's house, Chloe noticed many things seemed different in Haiti. They passed a lot of buildings that Chloe thought must be people's homes, and what looked to be little stores.

Every so often Chloe saw a goat walking along the side of the road, and some chickens, just walking around free to go wherever they wanted. Chloe thought that everything seemed so bright because it was so sunny out. It was also very hot. The car was going fast, and with the windows down the breeze felt good on Chloe's face.

They eventually drove through a downtown area of a city where there were many concrete buildings and people. Some people were carrying fruits and vegetables or other things as they were walking, and others were sitting around talking to each other in groups. As they drove along the road past the city, going toward her grandma's house, the road went along the ocean. There was nothing but sand, a few trees and the big blue ocean.

By that time, it was early in the afternoon and the sun was very bright over the water making beautiful sparkling light flashes on the small waves. It was all so interesting to Chloe, so different from what she was used to, and at the same time she felt happy. She was happy to be with her grandma in Haiti.

Chloe's grandma asked if Chloe wanted to go with her to work the next day. Her grandma told her that she is a cook at an elementary school. She cooks food for the kids to eat for lunch.

Chloe exclaimed, "Yes, I would love to go with you!" Chloe went with her grandma the next morning. Chloe did not know what to expect. Would it be the same as her school? When they pulled up to the school, Chloe noticed that it looked different from her school.

They parked in front of the school. The school building was shaped like a U, with the front door in the middle. To the left and right of the school, there were many small buildings and some larger ones.

Chloe's grandma said the smaller buildings were houses where many of the children lived, and a large building to the right of the school was a church.

Chloe then saw several kids heading toward the U-shaped school. They were smiling and talking to each other. Chloe noticed they were all dressed alike in uniforms. Chloe said, "Look Grandma, they have uniforms too." Chloe was excited to see the kids and to see that they also wore uniforms to school just like she did.

Chloe followed her grandma to a large kitchen area where there were several other ladies. They all worked together to prepare the food for the kids. Chloe's grandma said there are about sixty kids at the school, so they must make a lot of food. Chloe looked around the kitchen and saw all sorts of vegetables and meats.

Some looked familiar to her and others she had never seen before. Her grandma and the other ladies started to sing as they prepared the food. They worked hard and looked happy. Chloe was excited to be there with her grandma.

At lunchtime, the kids came out of the school and walked
over to the church. Chloe learned that this building was not
just a church, it was where the kids went to eat lunch.
Inside the church were many long wooden tables with
benches. Chloe followed her grandma and the other ladies
as they carried many bowls of food over to where the kids
were sitting at the tables. Three large bowls of food were
placed on each table, and the kids passed them
around. Chloe had not seen this kind of food before.

Her grandma asked Chloe if she would like to try some.
She took a spoonful from each bowl and put it on her plate,
just like she saw the other kids do. She hesitated just a bit,
and then took a bite of the food. She thought,
Wow, this is so good!

After eating, the kids went back to the school to finish the
day. Chloe helped her grandma clean up the lunch area,
and then they went back to the kitchen to clean up the
dishes. Chloe was really enjoying the day with her
grandma. Also, she thought it was so nice to see what
the kids in Haiti are like. Chloe thought to herself,
Wow, they are just like me.

In the afternoon, Chloe and her grandma walked around so Chloe could see more of the village. As they walked back near the school, it was time for recess and the kids were playing outside. Chloe saw several kids jumping rope and singing. Chloe exclaimed, "Grandma, they are jumping rope and singing just like I do!"

Her grandma asked if she would like to go play with them and Chloe nodded her head yes.

Chloe noticed their songs were in another language, and
she did not understand the words, but they seemed similar
to the songs she and her friends sang while jumping rope.
One of the kids motioned for Chloe to try it, and Chloe
started jumping rope. She sang the song she made up
before coming to Haiti, "One, two, three, headed to Haiti.
Five, six, seven, airplane goes high as Heaven. Eight, nine,
ten, going to Grandma's again."

The other kids then sang Chloe's song while jumping and
they helped Chloe learn one of their songs. Chloe had so
much fun jumping rope with them. She thought to herself,
Wow, they are just like me.

After recess the kids went back inside the school. Chloe helped her grandma for the rest of the day as her grandma prepared things for the next day. When school was over, the kids walked toward their houses in the village. Soon after, they came back outside andwere dressed just like Chloe.

Many of the kids went over to a grassy area where they started to play soccer. Chloe was so excited to see them playing a game that she knew how to play too. She looked up at her grandma and exclaimed, *Wow, Grandma, they are just like me!*

About an hour later, the kids went back to their houses. Chloe noticed that each house had a large porch area with a big table, and there were several kids on each porch. The kids ate dinner there and then began to work on their homework from school.

Chloe and her grandma took another walk around the village. As they walked past one of the houses, Chloe noticed several kids were working math problems just like she did at home. She waved to them and smiled. She thought to herself, *Wow, they are just like me.*

A little while later, Chloe saw many of the kids walking toward the church building. Chloe's grandma told her that most of the kids go to church in the evenings. Chloe and her grandma walked over to the church too. Chloe noticed that the long tables where they had eaten lunch had been moved to the side and there were just benches lined up in rows for the kids to sit on.

They sang many songs, just like she did at her church. Chloe thought to herself, *Wow, they really are just like me.*

Chloe had so much fun in Haiti with her grandma and loved seeing the kids. When it was time to go home, she gave her grandma a big hug. She said, "Grandma, thank you so much. I loved visiting Haiti. I hope to come back and visit soon."

When Chloe returned home, her friends asked her what the kids in Haiti were like. Chloe thought to herself for a little bit, and then she said, "Well, they wear uniforms to school just like I do. They jump rope and sing just like I do. They play soccer, do math homework and go to church just like I do." Then, she smiled and said, *"The kids in Haiti are just like me."*